DREAM TEAM!

DREAM TEAM!

JO STANLEY

FIVE
MILE

Five Mile, an imprint of
Bonnier Publishing Australia
Level 6, 534 Church Street,
Richmond, Victoria 3121
www.fivemile.com.au

First published 2017

National Library of Australia Cataloguing-in-Publication entry
Creator: Stanley, J. (Jo) author.
Title: Dream team! / Jo Stanley.
ISBN: 9781760409487 (paperback)
Series: Stanley, J. (Jo). Play like a girl.
Target Audience: For primary school age.
Subjects: Australian Football League.
Australian football teams
Women football players.
Friendship.
Schools.

For Willow

CHAPTER 1

BIGGEST. NEWS. EVER!

'Can you talk backwards?'

Hanh looked up from where she was sitting on the ground. 'Oh hi, Rainbow.' Hanh was getting ready for footy training and right now her attention was on her socks. She liked them to be as straight as possible, and exactly the same height on her shins. She always ran onto the field that way at the start of every quarter, and readjusted whenever she could, especially when she was taking a free kick. She was sure it made her play better.

'Can you talk backwards?' Rainbow asked again. 'I can. Nack ooyuh krawt sdaw-cab.' She sounded like an alien, in slow motion.

'What did you say?' Hanh asked impatiently.

'I said, can you talk backwards? Can – nack, you – ooyuh, talk – krawt—'

'Oh I get it,' Hanh interrupted, laughing. 'Funny! Or should I say,' Hanh imagined the word 'funny' written backwards in her head. It felt like she was doing mental yoga. 'Ee-nuf! Hey, funny backwards is "enough"!'

'COOL!' Rainbow said loudly. That was how she always spoke. Like someone had turned her volume up.

'But is it backwards if you're just saying the words, but not the *sentence* backwards?' Hanh asked.

Hanh watched Rainbow think for a moment and then shrug. 'That's the way I do it.'

Hanh stood up straight, finally happy with her sock arrangement. 'Want to run?'

'K.O!' Rainbow sprinted off. Hanh chased after her, grinning. Their warm-up lap always started this way, with a challenge to each other, and Hanh loved the race. It felt like just running next to someone, trying her hardest to win, lifted her heart beat and made her feet go faster.

The two girls both played in the midfield for their junior girls' footy team, the Flyers. Coach Shawna said that meant they should be connected, like acrobats. Rainbow had thought that meant they should do tricks, and non-stop cartwheeled the full length of the oval and nearly vomited. But Hanh understood. She had seen an acrobatic act in Cirque du Soleil, lifting and catching each other in perfect time. She and Rainbow needed to work together like that. And they did. When Hanh looked for someone to handball to, Rainbow was always there. When Rainbow took off out of the pack, Hanh was up ahead waiting for her. They were the perfect superhero duo.

Hanh was small, quiet and precise. Rainbow was tall, loud and goofy. They had played side by side in the Flyers for two years. Hanh couldn't imagine being on a footy field without Rai.

'RIGHTO!' Shawna's voice was a siren across the oval. The team gathered. 'FIRST THING. THE ROLE OF CAPTAIN. OF THE FLYERS. FOR THIS YEAR. IS UP FOR GRABS.'

Hanh was used to Shawna's deafening stop-start way of talking. It didn't matter how close they stood, she still yelled like her caps lock was stuck on. But this news made Hanh's stomach suddenly tighten.

'WE'RE NOW IN ROUND THREE. SO I WILL BE CHOOSIN'. THIS YEAR'S CAPTAIN.

AFTER THIS WEEKEND'S GAME. AGAINST THE JAGUARS.'

As Shawna spoke, the tightening in Hanh's stomach grew into a churning. She wanted to be captain more than anything she could think of. Last year when Mila was chosen, Hanh had burst into tears in front of the whole team. She still felt the burning embarrassment of it. But Mila had moved up to the Youth Girls division now and Hanh had been thinking about being captain since the start of the season. She could feel Maddie and Lucy looking at her, but she concentrated on Shawna's blue, spiky hair and tried to breathe calmly.

'I WILL BE LOOKIN' FOR PASSION, LEADERSHIP, COMMITMENT,' Shawna said.

Hanh felt so tense she feared she might push a fart out.

'AND SOMEONE. WHO LIFTS THE TEAM. WITH EVERYTHIN'. THEY. DO.' Shawna smiled broadly, then blasted her whistle. 'ALL RIIIIIIIGGGGHT!!! WE'RE SPRINTING!!!'

PASSION.

LEADERSHIP.

COMMITMENT.

The girls instantly spread out into a starting line and waited for Shawna's 'GO!'

It was a relief for Hanh to stretch her legs and arms. They were twitching to move.

'WHEN I SAY GO, YOU ARE RUNNING AWAY FROM A CHARGING CHEETAH. READY. SET. GOOOOOO!!!!'

Hanh always tried her absolute hardest, but now that she was racing to be captain, she pumped her arms and lifted her legs and listened to the in and out rhythm of her own puffing breath and pushed herself even harder. After an hour of training, she was exhausted, but happy. She gulped down a bottle of water.

'Your handballing is getting really fast,' Rainbow Gangnam-Styled up to her.

'Thanks,' said Hahn, wiping her mouth with the back of her hand. 'So is your marking.' Hanh smiled. Training always made her feel relaxed and light. 'Hey we're going for burgers. Wanna come?'

'Can't,' said Rainbow, matter-of-factly, 'I'm grounded.'

'What did you do now?' Hanh asked. She felt sorry for Rainbow. She wasn't naughty. She just didn't seem to know what was the right thing to do at the right time.

'All I did was write a chant for the Flyers.'

'That's OK, isn't it?'

'Except it was during Maths.'

'Oh,' Hanh screwed up her nose. *Wrong thing at the wrong time*, she thought. 'How did the chant go?'

'OK. Are you ready?

FLYERS ARE THE BEST

YOU BETTER RUN

WE'LL BE KICKING GOALS

YOU'LL BE SUCKING YOUR THUMB!'

Rainbow jumped up and down like a cheerleader.

Hanh laughed. 'Nice. But probably you should have been doing your maths.' Hanh loved maths, not just because she was good at it. She liked the way it made the world fit inside rules. Rainbow didn't like rules.

'Yeah, and then I kind of wrote it on my school desk, so I had to stay behind after school and scrub *all* the desks,' said Rainbow. Now she sounded sad.

'RAI!'

'I know. Gran was furious.' Rainbow lived with her gran, but she was more like a mum than a grandparent. She was warm and fun and laughed all the time, except when Rainbow was in trouble.

'Why did you write on your desk?' Hanh was shocked.

'BECAUSE I HATE SCHOOL! I'm just dumb at it!' Rainbow yelled.

Hanh wanted so badly to make Rainbow feel better, but she didn't know how.

'I just wanna play footy,' said Rainbow.

Hanh grinned at her. 'Well, you're awesome at that.'

'Thanks!' Rainbow swung her arm over Hanh's shoulders. 'We're awesome TOGETHER!'

I
JUST
WANNA
PLAY

FOOTY!

CHAPTER 2

ATTACK OF THE WORRY NINJA

The cafe was loud. Hanh sat crammed with Sarah, Maddie and Lucy around a table for two, while the parents sat at the next table. They ate crispy, salty chips and giant hamburgers, almost too big to bite, and sucked down soft drink noisily. It was delicious! 'How good is this?' Hanh licked the juice from her burger off her fingers. Her parents owned a Vietnamese restaurant, so all the dinners at home were steamed fish, hot stews, stir-fried veggies or rice. Other people told her she was SO lucky, but she thought it was boring. A hamburger and chips was gourmet to her.

'So,' Sarah said, in between stuffed mouthfuls, 'who do you think will be captain?'

Hanh put her hamburger down and wiped her hands. Her churning stomach had come back.

'It'll be you, Hanh, for sure,' Maddie said.

'Maybe,' Hahn said. 'I'd like to do it.' She felt nervous admitting it. The truth was, in the most secret part of her heart, Hanh thought she deserved to be captain. She was a good organiser and hadn't missed one game or training session in two years, even when she had a cold and a snot monster had taken over her head. She loved the Flyers and would do anything for the team.

'Yeah, like you know how you take warm-ups when Shawna is talking to the parents?' Maddie said.

Hanh nodded. She saw herself handballing to a line of players, one by one. It was nice to hear Maddie mention it.

'And remember your tackle in the Grand Final last year, when you saved that goal?' said Lucy.

'Yeah, we still got thrashed though.' Hanh remembered the heartbreak of that final siren.

'Would have been worse without you,' said Maddie.

'Ha! Obviously!' said Hanh. Her friends were being so nice, and saying such encouraging things. She started to feel big and bold.

'And remember how you printed the footy rules for me when I started this year?' Sarah added. 'That was a big help.'

Bit by bit, Hanh let her heart believe her wish could come true.

'Rainbow would be a good captain too, I think,' said Lucy.

Hahn looked at Lucy in surprise.

'She definitely works as hard as you,' Lucy continued, 'and she's one of our best players.'

Hahn took a gulp of her drink, sucking from her straw hard. It made a slurping noise at the bottom of the cup. Inside she was confused and cross. Rainbow was her friend and she didn't want to be mean, but how could anyone think *she* could be captain?

'And Rai lifts the team, like Shawna said. She made me feel so much better that time I missed the goal after the siren,' said Lucy.

'And she's SO funny,' added Sarah.

'Also,' said Lucy, 'she's REALLY enthusiastic.'

Hanh felt her heart drop. Suddenly she didn't believe she could be captain anymore.

'Where is she, by the way?' said Maddie.

'She's grounded. Again!' said Hahn. She wanted

to sound funny, and thought the others would laugh along with her. But they didn't. They were quiet. Hanh was even more confused. What she meant and what she was saying seemed to be all in a muddle, and everything was coming out sounding mean.

Lucy was the first to break the silence. 'Well, we'll find out next week, I guess.' She started clearing her rubbish. Sarah did the same. It was time to go home.

Hanh felt miserable.

'I still hope you get made captain, Hanh' said Maddie.

'Thanks Maddie,' said Hanh. 'So do I.'

There was one whole day of school to get through before the game against the Jaguars. Hanh tried not to think about football at all. But it kept popping into her head when she wasn't ready for it. And then she would be thinking about who would be captain, and she'd suddenly feel nervous and worried. It was like her brain was hijacked by a Worry Ninja.

In Maths, every number she looked at became a footy score, a combination of goals and behinds, until she forgot to do the task Miss Graham had set for them. In Science, gravity made her think about how a footy flies through the air and falls to the ground again, until she got caught not listening and Miss Graham moved her to sit right down the front. In Creative Writing, all her stories became about playing footy. Finally, Miss Graham banned any mention of football in her classroom for the rest of the year.

'Even us, Miss?' Sarah asked.

'Even you and Maddie and all of you footy-crazy girls!' Miss Graham nodded fiercely as she spoke. She was like an angry bobblehead toy.

Hanh felt bad. She loved school. She liked feeling smart and working hard. Year 5 was exciting, with lots of new ideas to understand. She loved stretching her mind to find an answer, and then the satisfying feeling of a new discovery. But today she had been acting dumb. She never wanted to have a day, or week, like this again. She couldn't wait to play the Jaguars and prove to Shawna that she could be captain, and then things could go back to being normal.

CHAPTER 3

THE FUMBLE SISTERS

Rainbow was walking through the carpark when Hanh arrived at the Jaguars' ground. Hanh thought Rai always looked as though she'd already played a game of footy. Her uniform was baggy and worn. She was in bare feet, carrying her socks and footy boots, even though it was spitting rain. Her hair was unbrushed. She had a knot in the back of it that Hanh wouldn't have been able to ignore on herself. But Rainbow didn't seem to notice or care.

Hanh ran over. It felt good to see her friend.

'Ready to kick some Jaguar butt?' Hanh said, holding her hand up for a high five.

'Yeah, but see they've lost the J off the front of their sign? So we're playing the Aguars!' Rainbow laughed loudly, as she met Hanh's high five. 'THE AGUARS!'

Hanh giggled, half at the sign and half at how funny Rainbow was. But inside her thoughts were all about who was going to be chosen as captain. It felt strange, behaving and feeling two different things.

Shawna took the team through warm-up in her

usual unusual way. Today, they lined up and danced the Can Can to warm up their kicking legs. Rainbow sang the *dah-dah da-da-da-da dah-dah* music at the top of her voice, and they all got puffed and giggly.

Hanh joined the line of high kicks, but really she wanted to volunteer to take the goal-kicking drill. She'd googled it that morning to prove that as captain she could help her team practise their skills. This silly warm-up annoyed her. How would it help them win?

In the team huddle, Shawna gave them one thing to remember during the match. She did this every game. Last week it was 'THE GROUND IS LAVA'. That game they felt like they ran super fast. The week before it was 'BE A PIMPLE ON THEIR BUM', which made them all laugh at how gross that was. But that game they tackled harder than ever before.

Today she said, 'DON'T HEAR FOOTSTEPS. WHAT DO I MEAN?'

Hanh put up her hand. 'I reckon the Jaguars—'

'You mean the AGUARS!' Rainbow interrupted.

The team laughed again.

Hanh continued, straining over the team's laughter. 'The Jaguars are really big and rough. So "Don't Hear Footsteps" means don't be scared. Like, don't look over your shoulder, keep your head down, be brave and play the ball... just be brave and play the ball as hard and fast as you can.'

'NICE ONE HANH!' Shawna clapped loudly and the team joined her. Hanh smiled broadly. It felt great to share her ideas and for Shawna to like them.

Rainbow put up her hand. Hanh was surprised. Rainbow hadn't done that before.

'I just wanted to say that I've written a chant that we all can do. It goes —

FLYERS FLY HIGH

CAUSE WE'VE HAD PRACTICE

JAGUARS ARE GONNA

SIT ON A CACTUS!

— I googled it,' Rainbow said. 'Jaguars live in Texas where there are lots of cactusses-es.'

The girls laughed and cheered and whooped. Together they chanted Rainbow's war cry.

Except Hanh. 'I think you mean cacti!' she called over the team's happy chanting, but no one cared. Hanh grew more annoyed. What the team needed was something to focus on, like being brave, not a stupid rhyme that didn't tell them anything about *how* to win.

The game started and Hanh and Rainbow played just like acrobats, except acrobats who had never rehearsed. They were like the worst act on Australia's Got Talent. *Ladies and Gentlemen, please welcome THE FUMBLE SISTERS!* Hanh thought Rainbow was going left when actually she went right and they ran straight into each other. Another time, Rainbow kicked to Hanh as she always did, smooth and controlled. But Hanh fumbled and missed like someone learning to juggle. She became frustrated, and then she became cross.

Sitting in the club rooms at half time, Hanh was furious. She was trying her hardest, but it was like a bad-playing spell had been cast on her. But Rainbow was having one of her best games ever, and Shawna was talking to her right now, as if they were sharing a secret. Had she chosen the captain already? Hanh started to panic. She had to make sure her second half was better than Rainbow's. But how?

The umpire bounced the ball to start the third quarter, and Tahani tapped it out of the centre for the Flyers. Hanh swooped and picked it up, looking around the pack. Rainbow was waving, calling to her in an open space clear of any Jaguars. She was the first and best option to pass to. But Hanh turned and handballed to Lucy. The ball moved forward quickly, leaving Rainbow out of play.

The next time Hanh had the ball, she did the same. And the next time, and the time after that. Every time, she acted like she didn't see Rainbow. Deep down she felt guilty. But on top of that feeling, she piled other thoughts. Thoughts like *I'm just playing the best I can, I'm allowed to pass to anyone I want, It's not my fault, Rainbow could play harder if she wanted* – but mostly *PLEASE LET SHAWNA CHOOSE ME.*

When the siren went, the Flyers had won by an easy 25 points. Yet as her teammates jumped up and down with their arms in the air, Hanh didn't feel like celebrating. Instead she felt like she needed to say sorry to Rainbow for being so selfish. It was a terrible dark feeling, but she pretended it wasn't there.

The girls made their way in twos and threes toward the club rooms on happy and exhausted wobbly legs. Hanh tried to smile. She knew Shawna was about to announce who would be captain of the Flyers this year, and all she could do was hope that it would be her.

WHO HAS BEEN
SELECTED AS
CAPTAIN
THIS YEAR?

CHAPTER 4

TREES SHOULDN'T TALK

The girls gathered in the cold grey concrete club rooms. They were muddy and tired, but elated they had beaten the Jaguars. There was a buzz of anticipation in the room.

Hanh squeezed in next to Sarah and Maddie. Her heart felt like it was beating faster than it should, and her breath felt shaky. This was the moment she had been looking forward to, but now was afraid of. She stood still and quiet, with her heart beating like she was doing the 100-metre sprint. *No matter what*, she thought, *do not cry*.

The girls, usually chatty and bubbly, hushed and waited. Finally, Shawna spoke in her usual stop-start, yelling way.

'LADIES, FANTASTIC JOB TODAY. GREAT WIN. NOW. WHO HAS BEEN SELECTED. AS CAPTAIN. THIS YEAR?'

Hanh tried to act like she didn't really care, which was hard because she wasn't very good at acting. She had been a tree in the school play of *The Wizard of Oz*, and had to stand still with no expression on her face. But in the middle of 'Somewhere Over The Rainbow' dust got up her nose and she'd sneezed loudly. The whole audience laughed at the sneezing tree and she ruined the whole scene. Now she tried to do her best 'I don't care, I'm just a tree' face.

Shawna continued. 'IT'S SOMEONE WHO ALWAYS WORKS HARD. SOMEONE WHO WOULD DO ANYTHING FOR THE CLUB. AND LIFTS THE TEAM. ON FIELD AND OFF.'

Hanh stood frozen. Even her chest and the lungs inside seemed to stop.

'THAT PERSON IS RAINBOW.'

Nineteen girls exploded into raucous cheering and whooping and clapping. The noise hit Hanh like a punch in the tummy. She felt the prickle of tears behind her eyes but, a few seconds later, she forced herself to smile and cheer.

Rainbow was swamped, as they all pushed in towards her to give her a hug. It was a bobbing sea of grins and guffaws.

Rainbow looked happier than Hanh had ever seen

her. She laughed loudly with every teammate, and said their names as if she was listing her favourite people. 'Thanks Tahani. Sarah – yes! Oh thanks, Lucy. Ruby, thank you.'

Shawna stood back against the wall, watching. Hanh glanced over to her. Shawna smiled, but Hanh couldn't smile back. It felt so unfair. How could she choose someone who always got in trouble and mucked around in training all the time?

Hanh wanted to run out of the club rooms and never come back. She shoved her footy boots in her bag and went over to Rainbow. Without dropping her bag from her shoulder, she gave her friend an awkward hug.

'Well done, Rainbow,' she said. Her voice sounded weak. *You see* that *is why they don't give me any lines to say in the play*, she thought. *Trees should never talk.*

'Thanks Hanh,' Rainbow squeezed her tightly.

Hanh hated it. She hated everything in the whole world right now. She needed to escape, to run away before she turned into The Hulk and everybody laughed at her stupid, sad green face.

CHAPTER 5

EXPLOSION!

Hanh burst through the restaurant door from the busy street. The heavy green plastic strips in the doorway made a slapping noise. Her mother followed behind her. Her brother Trai was standing behind the take-away counter.

'About time, Pea Brain,' he said. 'I'm going out tonight, you need to come serve.'

'No way! Mum?' Hanh turned to her mother to settle this.

'Trai, you have another hour on your shift,' their mother said calmly. Hanh had never heard her mum raise her voice. Her steady tone was like an anchor in their chaotic house.

'Ha! Stink Head!' Hanh stormed past Trai to the rabbit-warren house behind him. She wasn't in the mood for smiling at customers or selling dumplings or even being a normal human. She just wanted to be by herself, to be angry and hurt, and to cry.

Their house began at the back of the restaurant kitchen, and weaved its way through a lounge room, where Ong, her grandfather, sat almost permanently watching TV, past an office, bathroom and kitchenette, and up narrow stairs to their bedrooms. Hanh stomped through the house and shut herself in her room. It was tiny. There was only a bed, a desk, a wardrobe and a bookshelf, with only a strip of walk way between. But she didn't care. Their house was a constant bang, smash and holler of people, with Ong, her parents, Trai and her twin little brothers, Kim and Minh, all living there. This was the only place where she could close the door to the noise. She slammed it shut and burst into tears.

All around her, on the wall above her desk and over her bed, were memories of the Flyers, and all that they had done together. Photos of the fundraising bush dance, the special jumper they wore when they played in Sydney, the 'Well Done' card Shawna had given her at the end of the season last year. It all had made her feel proud and special. But now looking at it through wet, blurry eyes, she just felt like a loser. Maybe she wasn't as good at playing footy as she'd thought. Maybe Shawna never liked her. Maybe she was a hopeless, embarrassing, worst-player-on-the-team loser with a capital 'L' on her forehead.

She put her head in her hands, letting her tears drop onto the desk and the snot stream from her nose. It felt good to feel sorry for herself. She wanted to sit there alone, sobbing, forever.

But the door flung open and Kim and Minh tumbled into her room. They were dressed like mini Captain Americas and had a Nerf gun each.

'STICK 'EM UP!' they yelled. They aimed Nerf darts directly at Hanh. She was too sad and slow to defend herself against the tiny superheroes. A dart hit her on the chest, then another on her forehead, then one on her left cheek. She dodged a dart heading straight for her eyes just in time.

'Stop it! STOP IT!' she yelled, but the boys kept coming.

'Yeaah! YEAAH!' they cried. When they ran out of darts they threw their guns on the floor and launched themselves at Hanh.

'I SAID STOP IT!' Hanh yelled, louder than she

meant to. And then she pushed them both off her, harder than she meant to. Minh fell with a thud on the floor and Kim fell on top of him and then suddenly they were howling. Big heavy tear drops streamed down their faces.

Hanh felt terrible. Just because she was sad, she'd hurt her two brothers who she loved more than anything. She bent to pick them up and give them a cuddle, but she was interrupted by a loud ringing from downstairs. It was the signal from the restaurant that Trai needed her help. This was the worst day ever.

'NOOOO.' Hanh felt like she wanted to explode. There was so much heat flowing through her muscles and into her head it took all her self-control not to scream. All she wanted was to be alone, so that she could feel sad by herself. But no one was ever alone in her house. There was always the restaurant and the twins. And when she wasn't doing that she had school work and chores. It felt like every part of her life was pressing down on her.

Hanh picked Minh and Kim up, one by one, and dumped them on her bed. She flopped down between them, and put her arms around their tiny shoulders. They instantly snuggled into her and their crying calmed down.

She took a big deep breath in and out again, listening to the sound of the air through her nose and feeling it escape out of her nostrils, the way they had learned at school. The heat started to subside. Now she just felt empty and flat, like she was a toy that had run out of batteries. There were so many confusing thoughts in her head, she started to list them:

* *Fact*: she shouldn't have yelled at Minny and Kimmy. *Feeling*: guilty and mean.

* *Fact*: she shouldn't have stopped passing to Rainbow in the game today. *Feeling*: double guilty and mean.

* *Fact*: she didn't get chosen as captain of the Flyers. *Feeling*: sad and like a complete loser.

The problem was, now that she had listed those thoughts and feelings, she didn't know what to do with them. It was all such a jumble in her head and even more mixed up in her heart. Rainbow was her friend. She loved playing with her. *But why did she have to get Captain instead of me?* Hanh thought. *It's not fair.*

The restaurant bell rang again, and Hanh gave a big sigh. She kissed Minh and Kim on the forehead.

'I love you,' she said, squeezing them tight.

The boys wriggled away and jumped up and down on her bed, as though there had been no tears only moments before. Hanh laughed. 'No jumping on the bed, remember!' she said, knowing her mum would be cross, except she didn't really mean it. She loved their cheeky fun. It was the sunshine in her stormy day.

CHAPTER 6

A

MYSTERY

'**H**ey Hanh, wanna play kick-to-kick?' Sarah was hanging upside down on the monkey bars. Maddie was sitting on top next to her. Sarah swung up to sitting as she spoke. 'Isaac and Max just went to get a footy.'

Hanh screwed up her face in disappointment. She hated missing out. But she had a very special job to do, and she felt important doing it.

'Can't. I'm going to a Student Rep meeting.' Hanh was working with the Student Representative Council at their neighbouring school, Milsborough Central Primary School, to organise a walking school bus route they could share. This lunchtime, Miss Graham was taking her to meet with their Student Rep, Archie.

'How cool!' Maddie jumped down from the monkey bars.

Hanh watched as Sarah dismounted next to her. 'Take a specky on Maxy's back for me!' she called after them. Sarah and Maddie laughed.

School was Hanh's second-favourite place, after

the footy field. She liked that she knew everyone, had lots of friends and did lots of interesting things. But especially this week, when she felt a twinge of sadness every time she remembered Rainbow was captain and she wasn't, all the fun things she did helped her feel better.

On Monday, she beat a Grade 6 boy in chess club. On Tuesday, she served an ace in before-school tennis. On Wednesday, she learned a new piece in piano. Even at Thursday night footy training, the SRC meeting gave her a different thing to think about when watching Rainbow as captain made her feel gloomy. Now she was visiting this school to plan something that was special for lots of kids in their neighbourhood. It made being the captain of the Flyers seem like a smaller thing.

It was odd, walking through a school that was so close to her own, but different. She felt like a stranger there. The only student she really knew at the school was Rainbow, and Hanh hadn't told her she would be there. She hadn't said very much to her at all that week.

When the meeting was finished, Archie took her through the playground to the front gates, and Hanh saw Rainbow, on the other side of the asphalt. She was standing by herself under a tree, scratching something into the bark with a stick.

Hanh stopped for a moment. She waved, but Rainbow didn't see her. She looked around to see who Rainbow was playing with. There were no other kids anywhere. Hanh wondered if her friends had gone to the tuck shop or if they were all playing Hide and Seek, or Truth or Dare. She hoped so.

For the rest of the day, the Worry Ninja kept reminding Hanh of seeing Rainbow alone in the playground, and when it did, she felt sad. It was a relief to have jobs to distract her, like feeding Kim and Minh their dinner, which was always tricky. It was like feeding two cheeky monkeys at the zoo. They were wriggly and messy and naughty and chatty. This night, Hanh let their non-stop chattering giggles take her away from football and the Flyers and Rainbow.

'More noodles!' said Kim.

'Noodle oodle oodle woodle,' said Minh.

'Woodle noodle poodle,' said Kim.

'Poodle noooooooodles!' squealed Minh.

They both squealed at their joke. Hanh didn't see what they were laughing at, but laughed at their laughter. It was so silly and fun. It was the first time this week she'd laughed freely like that, and it felt good. She let herself giggle away with the twins, like being carried along on a wave.

CHAPTER 7

HORSESHOE CREEK

Saturday morning was quiet in Hanh's house. The restaurant was closed, so Hanh had some precious time for herself before the Flyers' footy match.

This day, she wandered out the back door and into the cobblestone laneway behind their house. She loved to meander through the connecting alleys that wove their way like an ant nest from one side of Milly West to the other. Finally, she stopped at the edge of Horseshoe Creek.

Horseshoe Creek wasn't much of a creek. It was a trickle of water that flowed off the wide and brown Kulin River that wound its way through the middle of Milly West like a spine. The Kulin was big and popular. You could ride boats on it or fish. Horseshoe Creek was not useful to anyone, except for ducks, frogs and local kids, lost in their games and imagination.

Hanh picked her way carefully down a track that had been worn into the long grass and overgrown bushes. From the street you had to look carefully to even find it. But once you pushed past the first clump of tall weeds, it was clear where to go, thanks to all the footsteps that had been there before. And then, down a steep and sometimes slippery path, was a mossy, rocky and muddy creek bed. It was shaded by tall gum trees and was lovely and cool in summer – although you had to be careful of snakes. Today though, it was shivery cold. It had rained overnight, and there was more water flowing in the creek than normal.

Hanh sat on a big boulder and threw pebbles, one by one, into the water. She was surrounded by a wall of wild blackberry bushes on one side, and a muddy steep rock on the other. It was quiet and still. She imagined she had created her own secret hideaway.

The *tip tap* of spitting rain started again on the leaves above Hanh. She stood up to leave, and then froze. Over the blackberry bushes and down the creek, she could see a girl. It was Rainbow. She was holding on to an overhanging tree branch with one hand, and reaching for something in the water with the other. Hanh quickly crouched down. She peered through the blackberry bush to see what Rainbow was doing.

'Come on, little guy,' Rainbow was saying gently.

Not far from the end of Rainbow's stretching hand, there was something light grey and fluffy splashing around in the water and making a high-pitched squeaking noise.

'You can do it, little guy.' Rainbow carefully took another step towards the splashing. The branch she was holding bent sharply.

Hanh craned her neck to get a better look. She could see there was a duckling, or maybe a baby swan in the water. It was hard to tell. But the answer came with an angry honk, when a big black swan appeared at the top of the embankment, high above Rainbow.

Rainbow jumped at the sound of the mother swan. The branch she was holding onto cracked and Rainbow lost her balance. She waved her free arm around in the air, trying to steady herself, but the swan's honking got louder and angrier.

Without thinking, Hanh jumped up from her hiding spot and yelled, 'RAI, LOOK OUT!'

She slid off her boulder and splish-splashed her way over to Rainbow as fast as the rocky muddy creek bed would let her.

The swan flapped fiercely down the embankment towards Rainbow, honking like a speeding truck. Rainbow tried to pull herself back on to her dry patch, but the branch snapped and she fell into the creek, face first. The swan launched herself towards Rainbow.

As Rainbow shielded her head with her arms, Hanh pulled her out of the shallow water by her waist. The two girls staggered away from the furious bird and collapsed on a soft grassy outcrop.

The swan stopped honking. She waddled over to her baby, who was still squeaking and splashing away in its own little rock pool. She turned and sat in front of the cygnet, and it hopped up on to her back. Finally, the squeaking stopped. The mother picked her way over the rocks and puddles and mud of the riverbed to where the water was deeper, and gracefully sailed off in the direction of the Kulin River, her baby snuggling in safely under her wing.

Hanh and Rainbow looked at each other and laughed. Rainbow was soaked and filthy down one side of her body, and Hanh's shoes were all muddy.

'Are you OK?' Hanh said.

'Yep!' Rainbow said, still laughing. 'What are you doing here?'

'Just came down here to be alone.'

'Oh.' Rainbow nodded. 'I was trying to save that baby swan. They don't normally come down here. I guess it was lost.'

Hanh thought about how caring Rainbow was. And then in her mind she saw her at school standing under the tree by herself.

'I saw you at school yesterday,' Hanh said, picking wet leaves off Rainbow's top.

'Really?' Rainbow sounded confused.

'I was there for SRC,' Hanh explained. 'Who were you playing with?'

Rainbow shrugged, and then looked away down the creek. 'Everyone plays downball.'

'Don't you play?' Now it was Hanh's turn to sound confused.

'Nah, it's stupid! Anyway, they don't like the way I play,' Rainbow sniffed. 'I just do my own thing.'

Hanh played downball at school sometimes, and loved it. And she always had lots of friends to hang out with. But Rainbow didn't even have anyone from the Flyers at her school. Hanh suddenly felt sad.

'Well done on being Captain,' she said.

'Thanks,' said Rainbow. 'It's the best thing that has EVER happened to me!'

Hanh looked at Rainbow's face. She had a nasty red bruise on her cheek, but somehow she was still smiling, a silly grubby beaming smile. Hanh gave her a hug. A hug that said *you're awesome*. A hug that said *I'm so glad you're my friend and I think you'll be a great captain*. A hug that said *forgive me for being the stupidest nastiest jealous green monster around*.

'Come on,' Hanh said. 'We've got a footy match to play.'

Rainbow grinned. 'YESSS! You can tell everyone how you saved me from a killer swan.'

WE'VE GOT A FOOTY MATCH TO PLAY!

CHAPTER 8

BFFS

Hanh stood looking down at her socks with satisfaction. They were sitting exactly at the same height as each other on her shins. She'd had so many topsy-turvy emotions in the last two weeks, it was a relief to feel neat, ordered and ready to play the Tigers.

'Nice socks!' Shawna was standing in front of her, grinning. 'I would say they're a real SOCKS-ESS!! Get it? SOCKS-ESS!!' She roared at her own joke.

Hanh put her hands over her ears, pretending to be in pain from the bad pun. 'Ow, my ears!' she groaned. But then laughed, and added, 'Your jokes sock, Shawna!'

Shawna shrieked, open-mouthed, at Hanh's gag. It made Hanh laugh harder.

'So.' Shawna was suddenly serious. 'I guess you wish I had chosen you for Captain.'

Hanh screwed up her face. She didn't really want to talk about it. It made her feel bad, just thinking about the game against the Jaguars. Hanh wanted to forget the whole day happened. 'It's OK. Rainbow will be really good.' Hanh meant what she said, even though she felt sad saying it.

'She will be. She loves this club more than anythin'. It's her life. But you know – you don't have to have a C next to your name to be a leader.' Shawna concentrated very hard on Hanh's face when she spoke. She always did that.

Hanh nodded, even though that was the first time she'd thought about it. She really liked helping the other girls, and organising and researching drills. It was nice to hear from Shawna she could still do that. It made her feel like she was an important part of the team.

Shawna paused, looking out across the footy oval. The Tigers were gathering for their warm-up.

'Have you ever seen a mother bird teach her baby how to fly?' Shawna asked.

Hanh shook her head. She did NOT want to hear one of Shawna's weird stories. She wanted to run and kick and feel the ball between her hands.

'She pushes the baby out of the nest. The baby falls, thinkin' it can't fly. But then suddenly, it flaps its wings and – WOO HOO, it's FLYIN'!' Shawna flapped her arms excitedly. Hanh screwed her face up again, waiting for what Shawna was saying to make sense. 'Some people,' Shawna continued, 'don't know what they can be, till they're given the chance to be it.'

Hanh understood. Rainbow never got the chance to fly at school, but when she was at footy, she had the biggest wings. Hanh looked over at Rainbow, who was gathering the team around her on the field. She could hear Rainbow's booming voice.

'HERE WE GO, FLYERS
WE'RE HERE TO WIN,
WE'LL MAKE THE TIGERS
EMPTY THE BINS!'

The girls around her laughed. 'OK, how are we feeling? Luce, I know you've got a cold, let us know if you're struggling, OK? And Tahani, the Tigers' ruck is seriously big so we'll be keeping an eye out for you, OK? Are we ready? Let's RUN!'

The girls gave a round of applause, and then took

off for their warm-up.

Hanh took off after them. It was great to be running. She felt strong and happy. As she caught up with the group, she fell into rhythm with their footsteps. She loved being a part of those 40 feet, all running together. It made her feel like they could do anything.

When Rainbow went in to the centre for the coin toss, Hanh expected to feel sad it wasn't her. But instead, when the Flyers won the toss, Hahn was proud that Rainbow was their captain. And then when she danced, Gangnam Style, back to her place on the field, Hanh laughed and clapped and shouted 'woo hoo' loudly. She heard her opponent mutter 'what the?' under her breath. Rainbow had them fooled that she was easy to beat – and that was perfect.

When Hanh crouched, waiting for the opening siren to go, she grinned across at Rainbow. Opposite, Rainbow returned her smile. They were ready, for anything, together, as partners.

The umpire held the ball in the air, then bounced

it to start the game. Tahani reached high and tapped it down in the direction of Rainbow. Hanh darted out of the pack, shrugging a tackle on her left. Rainbow handballed towards her. Hanh picked up the ball and bounced, then passed it back to Rainbow, who chipped it to Lucy in their forward line.

Maddie, always faster than any girl playing on her, ran out into space in the forward pocket. Lucy kicked directly into Maddie's open arms, and Maddie held onto the ball in the way Shawna had shown her, like it was her favourite teddy. Taking her free kick, Maddie aimed calmly.

As the ball sailed through the goal posts, Hanh and Rainbow ran to each other and hugged.

'Perfect handball,' Rainbow said.

'Awesome kick,' Hanh replied.

'Should we do that again?' Rainbow fist bumped her, beaming.

'You bet,' Hanh called out, as she ran to stand beside her player, 'CAPTAIN!'

COLLECT THE OTHER BOOKS IN THE PLAY LIKE A GIRL SERIES!

Can't get enough of
PLAY LIKE A GIRL?
Here's a teaser from
TOTALLY EPIC!
Available from all
good bookstores!

Rainbow stuffed an orange quarter in her mouth. It was the middle of their Thursday-night footy training and the girls were all dipping into a container of cut up oranges and apples.

'My brother's started playing lacrosse,' said Lucy.

Rainbow smiled, showing orange peel instead of teeth.

Lucy giggled. 'And do you know what my dad said to him?'

'Mmmfmf rimfrffmfmnn rimfmfmmmmrr.' Rainbow tried to talk with her orange peel teeth. It was taking all of her control not to laugh.

'He said, "Why are you playing La *Cross*? You should play La Happy!"'

Rainbow couldn't hold her laugh in any longer. The orange peel burst out of her mouth and flew across the group of girls to land two metres away. Wiping her messy face with the back of her hand, Rainbow wondered if there was a world record in orange peel spitting, because she was pretty sure she had come close to breaking it.

Footy training was Rainbow's second-favourite part of the week. Of course her first-favourite part was Saturdays, when they played their games and she got to lead her footy team, the Flyers, out on to the field as their captain. But it didn't matter whether they were training or playing, being a part of the team meant this – laughing and mucking around, and never feeling weird or dumb. At school she felt like that all the time. But not with the Flyers. At footy, she could shout silly things and make up rhymes, like: CHEWY ON YOUR BOOT, SWALLOW A FLUTE, SWAP YOUR FOOTY JUMPER FOR YOUR BIRTHDAY SUIT! She could chase pigeons, do cartwheels or play Truth or Dare and always choose Dare.

'OK, FRUIT TINGLES!' Shawna yelled, even though she was standing right in the middle of their group. Rainbow and the other girls jumped to attention.

Shawna pulled out an iPad. 'RIGHT. THESE ARE. THE BEST MARKS. EVER TAKEN IN FOOTY.'

FOOTY CARDS

★

PLAYER PROFILES

HANH

Favourite colour:
RED

Favourite food:
hamburgers (not
that I get to eat
them EVER!)

Favourite saying:
HOW GOOD IS THIS?

Star sign:
ARIES

Favourite position:
WING

MILSBOROUGH WEST
FLYERS

RAINBOW

Favourite colour:
GREEN

Favourite food:
LOLLIES

Favourite saying:
HAH-YAH!

Star sign:
SAGITTARIUS

Favourite Position:
WING

MILSBOROUGH WEST
FLYERS

MADDIE

Favourite colour:
ORANGE

Favourite food:
ROAST CAULIFLOWER

Favourite saying:
HAVE A KICK!

Star sign:
TAURUS

Favourite position:
FULL FORWARD

MILSBOROUGH WEST
FLYERS

SARAH

Favourite colour:
GREYISH-PURPLE –
THE COLOUR OF
A STORM OVER
THE SEA

Favourite food:
FISH'N'CHIPS

Favourite saying:
SO COOL!

Star sign:
PISCES

Favourite Position:
BACK POCKET

MILSBOROUGH WEST
FLYERS

SHAWNA

COACH

Favourite colour:
BLUE

Favourite food:
ROAST LAMB

Favourite saying:
NO PRINCESSES!

Star sign:
**WHO HAS TIME FOR
THIS RUBBISH?**

Favourite position:
**THE MIDDLE OF
A HUDDLE AT
THREE-QUARTER
TIME**

MILSBOROUGH WEST
FLYERS